First published in Great Britain in 2018 by Pat-a-Cake
Pat-a-Cake is a registered trade mark of Hodder & Stoughton Limited
This book is based on the TV series PJ MASKS © Frog Box/Entertainment
One UK Limited/Walt Disney EMEA Productions Limited 2014
Les Pyjamasques by Romuauld © (2007) Gallimard Jeunesse.
All Rights Reserved
This book/publication © Entertainment One Limited 2018
Adapted by 38a The Shop. Text by Anne Marie Ryan.
ISBN: 978 1 52638 110 1 – 10 9 8 7 6 5 4 3 2 1
Pat-a-Cake, an imprint of Hachette Children's Group,
Part of Hodder & Stoughton Limited
Carmelite House, 50 Victoria Embankment, London EC4Y 0DZ
An Hachette UK Company
www.hachette.co.uk – www.hachettechildrens.co.uk
Printed and bound in China
A CIP catalogue record for this book is available from the British Library

# Save the Day

## CATBOY

has Super Cat Speed and drives the Cat-Car.

## OWLETTE

has Owl Wing Wind and flies in the Owl Glider.

## GEKKO

has Super Gekko Muscles and pilots the Gekko-Mobile.

## NIGHT NINJA

is a karate-whiz
and has an army
of Ninjalinos.

## ROMEO

is a super-brainy
villain with a Lab
and a robot helper.

## LUNA GIRL

flies around on her
Luna Board with
her flock of moths.

# CONTENTS

# STORY ONE
## Catboy and the Shrinker

# Chapter One
## CATBOY GETS SHRUNK

Connor was excited. He was finally tall enough to go in the big section of the playground! But when Connor, Amaya and Greg arrived everything had shrunk. Even the swings were tiny!

"We need to find out who's

done this!" said Connor.

That night, Connor and his friends turned into the PJ Masks. Connor transformed into Catboy. Amaya became Owlette. Greg turned into Gekko. The PJ Masks jumped into the Cat-Car and zoomed out of the tower.

As they drove around town, the PJ Masks saw that lots of other things had shrunk.

FLASH! Green light was coming from the park. They went to look around.

Romeo and Night Ninja drove up in a strange vehicle. It had a hose on top.

"Are you two shrinking things?" asked Owlette.

"I invented the Shrinker," Romeo said proudly.

"But I point the hose," said Night Ninja. He aimed the hose at a bench and light shot out. Now the bench was little!

"Stop that!" cried Catboy.

"OK," said Romeo. "It was just practice anyway."

"What we really want to shrink is YOU!" cried Night Ninja.

"Nobody is shrinking me!" shouted Catboy. He charged bravely at the baddies.

ZAP! The Shrinker's light hit Catboy. Now, he was as tiny as a kitten.

## Chapter Two

# A LITTLE LEADER

"Oh no! This is terrible!" squeaked Catboy. Even his voice was little!

"Now two more to go!" cried Romeo.

"When you're little, you won't be able to stop us from taking over the world!" said Night Ninja.

The baddies tried to shrink Owlette and Gekko, but the heroes moved too fast. Gekko sprinted away. Owlette flew after him with Catboy.

"Don't worry," Gekko told Catboy. "We'll help you."

"I don't need help!" squeaked
Catboy. "I'm small but I can
still be your leader. I'll prove it!"

Catboy tried to drive the
Cat-Car but his legs were too
short. He couldn't reach the pedals.

"Maybe I should drive,"
said Gekko.

ZOOM! The Cat-Car sped
around and around the villains.

"Woah!" groaned Romeo.

"I feel dizzy!" wailed
Night Ninja.

Catboy jumped out of the
Cat-Car and climbed onto
the Shrinker.

It was too big for him to control.
The Shrinker started moving.

"Yikes!" Catboy flew into
the air.

ZAP! Light from the Shrinker's
hose hit Catboy again. Now,
he was even smaller!

Owlette used her Super Owl Eyes to find Catboy hidden in the grass. He was so tiny he fitted in the palm of her hand!

"This is all my fault," wailed Catboy. "Being small makes me useless."

"You're not useless," said Owlette.

"Yes, I am!" squeaked Catboy sadly. "I'm practically invisible!"

Suddenly, Catboy had a great idea. "Wait!" he cried. "Maybe that could be useful . . ."

## Chapter Three
## CATBOY'S PLAN

Back in the park, Romeo and Night Ninja were squabbling over who was in charge. As the baddies argued, Owlette and Gekko sneaked up on them.

"Hand over the hose!" demanded Owlette.

Romeo tried to shrink
Owlette as she soared through
the air. Night Ninja's helpers,
the Ninjalinos, grabbed Gekko.
Catboy was so teeny, Night
Ninja didn't notice him climbing
up his body.

"Hee hee!" giggled Night
Ninja. "Something's tickling me."
He dropped the hose.

Gekko used his Super
Muscles to break free from the
Ninjalinos. He grabbed the
hose. Owlette pressed the reverse
button on the Shrinker's controls.

ZAP! Green light hit Catboy.

"Yes!" cheered Catboy.

He was back to his normal size!

Owlette pressed a different button. ZAP! ZAP! ZAP!

Gekko shrank the Ninjalinos.

"Run!" shouted Romeo.
He and Night Ninja ran away before they got shrunk too!

"Good work, PJ Masks," said Catboy. "Now we need to put everything back to the right size."

They drove the Shrinker around town, zapping everything that had been shrunk.

When they were done, Catboy said, "Now let's shrink the Shrinker."

"Hooray!" cheered the PJ Masks as the Shrinker vanished.

The next day, the friends went back to the playground.

"Are you going in the big section, Connor?" asked Amaya.

"No," said Connor. "I'll stay with you guys. Let's play here, before I'm too big for it!"

# STORY TWO
## Owlette the Winner

# Chapter One
## AMAYA WINS!

Amaya and her friends were playing basketball. In the last seconds of the game, Amaya caught the ball. She closed her eyes and tossed the ball in the air.

"Yay!" Everyone cheered. Amaya's lucky shot had won the game!

"I'm a winner!" sang Amaya. It felt great!

The referee tried to blow his

whistle but it was missing.

"We'll help you look for it," said Connor.

They searched everywhere, but the only thing they found was a moth.

"Luna Girl was here!" said Amaya.

"Why would she want a whistle?" wondered Greg.

That night, they turned into the PJ Masks.

"First one to track down Luna Girl wins!" said Owlette.

"You're on!" cried Catboy.

"HA HA HA!"

Catboy's Super Cat Ears heard Luna Girl laughing.

Owlette's Owl Eyes spotted Luna Girl on a rooftop.

"There she is!" said Owlette, pointing. "I win!"

"I heard her first," said Catboy. "So I win!"

"Let's call it a draw," said Gekko.

Owlette wasn't happy with that.

"First one to the top of the building wins," said Owlette.

"Get ready to lose," said Catboy.

Owlette flew up. Catboy climbed up. They reached the roof at the same time.

When Gekko got there, his friends were arguing about who had won.

"It doesn't matter who won," he told them.

"BLEEEEEP!"

The PJ Masks could ALL hear the whistle!

## Chapter Two
# MOTH THIEVES

The PJ Masks spied on Luna Girl. She was using the whistle to train two teams of moths. There was a big pile of toys on the roof.

"Soon every toy in the world will be mine!" said Luna Girl.

"The team that brings back the biggest toy wins."

She blew the whistle. The first team of moths flew off and brought back a toy car.

Luna Girl blew the whistle again. The second team stole a dinosaur.

"Slithering serpents!" said Gekko. "We can't let Luna Girl take all the toys."

"We've got to get the whistle," said Catboy. "Then the moths won't know what to do."

"First one to get the whistle

wins," said Owlette.

"That will be me," said
Gekko. "I can use my Super
Gekko Camouflage."

"No way," said Owlette.
"My owl wings will help me
win easily."

Gekko crept up behind
Luna Girl and tickled her. She
dropped the whistle. But before
Gekko could grab it, Owlette
swooped down.

CRASH!

Gekko and Owlette bumped into each other. Luna Girl snatched the whistle back.

"Ha ha!" Luna Girl said. "I win!" She flew off on her Luna Board. The moths followed, carrying the stolen toys.

"Wriggling Reptiles!" wailed Gekko. "Now what do we do?"

## Chapter Three
## THREE WINNERS

"Let's go to the toy shop," said Catboy. "And stop the moths."

"Whoever uses the coolest moves to get there wins," said Owlette. "Watch this!" She flapped her wings and did a flip.

"Check out my Super Lizard

Grip!" said Gekko. He climbed
down the side of the building.

"Look at my Super Cat Jumps!"
called Catboy. He leaped down
to the ground.

The PJ Masks each thought
their own moves were the coolest.

"I'm the winner!" cheered Owlette.

As Owlette did a victory dance, Luna Girl trapped Gekko and Catboy with her Luna Magnet.

"Oh no!" cried Owlette.

"This is all my fault!"

It was time to be a hero!

"Hey, Luna Girl!" called Owlette. "I bet your moths aren't strong enough to bring back the dinosaur in the toy shop window."

Luna Girl blew the whistle and her moths flew off. One team dropped a toy elephant onto the pile. The other team brought back a toy hippo.

"You fools!" cried Luna Girl. "You were supposed to bring me the dinosaur!" But the moths didn't know how to work together.

The pile of toys toppled over. It fell on Luna Girl. Gekko and Catboy were free!

"I'm sorry I made everything into a competition," Owlette told her friends.

"Let's get that whistle back together," said Catboy.

Catboy climbed up. "Hey, Luna Girl!" he called.

When Luna Girl turned to look, Gekko crept up behind her and grabbed the whistle. Then he threw it to Owlette.

"Game over, Luna Girl!" said Owlette.

"Now let's bring those toys back," said Catboy.

The PJ Masks saved the day by working together. They were all winners!